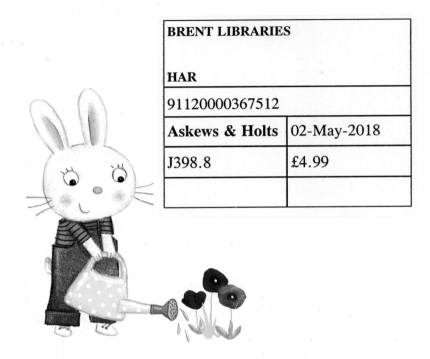

BRENT LIBRARIES	
HAR	
91120000367512	
Askews & Holts	02-May-2018
J398.8	£4.99

First published in Great Britain in 2018 by Pat-a-Cake
Copyright © Hodder & Stoughton Limited 2018. All rights reserved
Pat-a-Cake is a registered trade mark of Hodder & Stoughton Limited
ISBN: 978 1 52638 094 4 • 10 9 8 7 6 5 4 3 2 1
Pat-a-Cake, an imprint of Hachette Children's Group,
Part of Hodder & Stoughton Limited
Carmelite House, 50 Victoria Embankment, London EC4Y 0DZ
An Hachette UK Company
www.hachette.co.uk • www.hachettechildrens.co.uk
Printed in China

Playtime
Rhymes

Illustrated by Sharon Harmer

pat a cake

Pat-a-Cake

Pat-a-cake, pat-a-cake, baker's man.

Bake me a cake as fast as you can.

Pat it and prick it and mark it with 'B',

And bake it in the oven for baby and me.

Humpty Dumpty

Humpty Dumpty sat on a wall,
Humpty Dumpty had a great fall.
All the king's horses,
And all the king's men,
Couldn't put Humpty
Together again.

The Wheels on the Bus

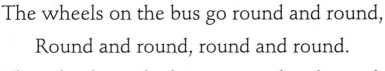

The wheels on the bus go round and round,
Round and round, round and round.
The wheels on the bus go round and round,
All day long.

The wipers on the bus go swish, swish, swish . . . all day long.

The horn on the bus goes beep, beep, beep . . . all day long.

The doors on the bus go open and shut . . . all day long.

The Grand Old Duke of York

Oh, the Grand old Duke of York,

He had ten thousand men.

He marched them up to the top of the hill,

And he marched them down again.

When they were up, they were up.
And when they were down, they were down.
And when they were only halfway up,
They were neither up nor down!

Baa, Baa, Black Sheep

Baa, baa, black sheep,
Have you any wool?
Yes sir, yes sir, three bags full!
One for the master, one for the dame,
And one for the little boy
Who lives down the lane.

Jack and Jill

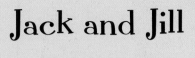

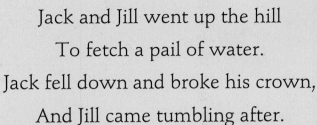

Jack and Jill went up the hill
To fetch a pail of water.
Jack fell down and broke his crown,
And Jill came tumbling after.

Up Jack got and home did trot,
As fast as he could caper.
He went to bed to mend his head,
With vinegar and brown paper.

Old MacDonald had a Farm

Old MacDonald had a farm, E-I-E-I-O.
And on that farm he had a cow, E-I-E-I-O.
With a moo, moo here, a moo, moo there,
Here a moo, there a moo, everywhere a moo, moo.
Old MacDonald had a farm, E-I-E-I-O.

And on that farm he had a sheep, E-I-E-I-O . . .
And on that farm he had a duck, E-I-E-I-O . . .
And on that farm he had a hen, E-I-E-I-O . . .
And on that farm he had a horse, E-I-E-I-O . . .

Baa,
baa!

Quack,
quack!

Cluck,
cluck!

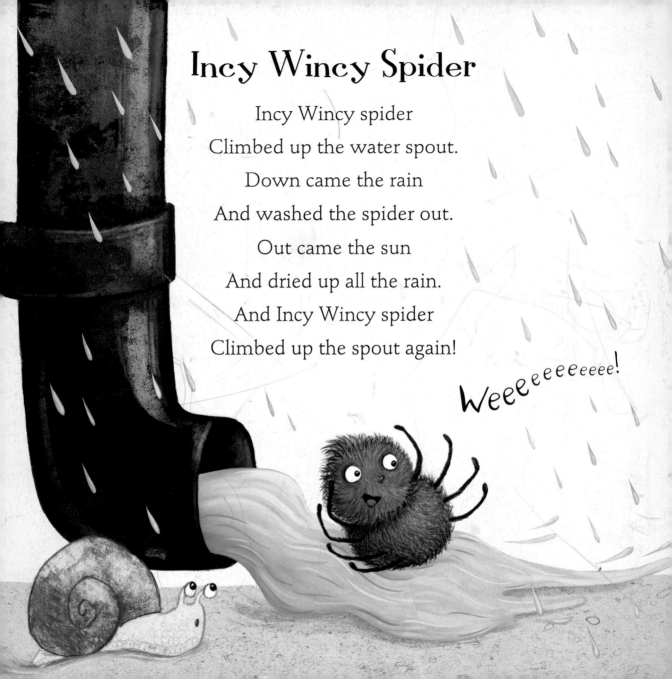

Incy Wincy Spider

Incy Wincy spider
Climbed up the water spout.
Down came the rain
And washed the spider out.
Out came the sun
And dried up all the rain.
And Incy Wincy spider
Climbed up the spout again!

Weeeeeeeeee!

Little Bo Peep

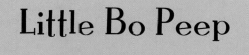

Little Bo Peep has lost her sheep,
And doesn't know where to find them.
Leave them alone and they'll come home,
Bringing their tails behind them.

Five Little Speckled Frogs

Five little speckled frogs,

Sat on a speckled log,

Eating the most delicious bugs (yum yum).

One jumped into the pool,

Where it was nice and cool,

Then there were four green speckled frogs (glub glub).

Four little speckled frogs . . .

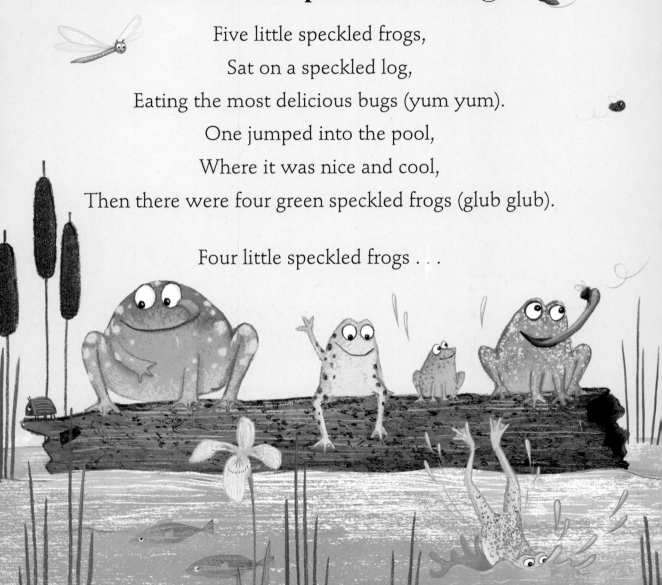

Little Miss Muffet

Little Miss Muffet
Sat on a tuffet,
Eating her curds and whey.
Along came a spider,
Who sat down beside her,
And frightened Miss Muffet away.

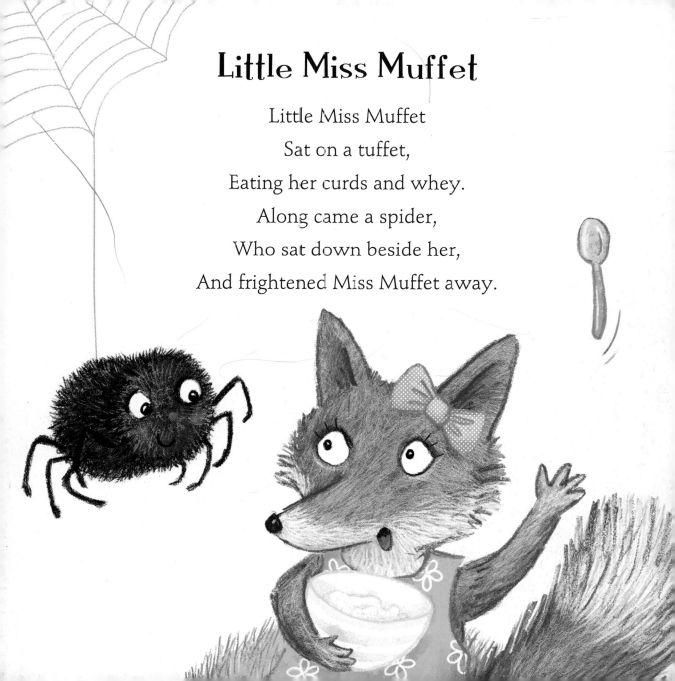

Row, Row, Row Your Boat

Row, row, row your boat
Gently down the stream.
Merrily, merrily, merrily, merrily,
Life is but a dream.

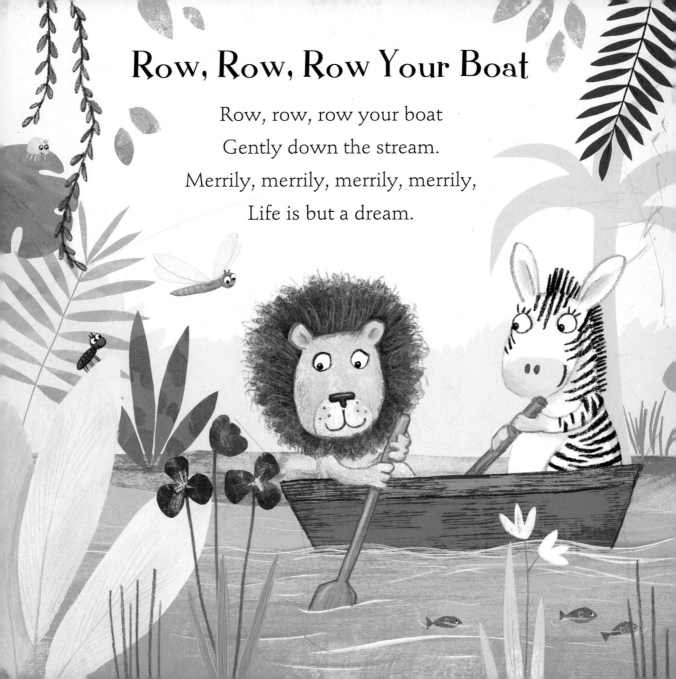

Row, row, row your boat
Gently down the stream.
If you see a crocodile,
Don't forget to scream!

Miss Polly had a Dolly

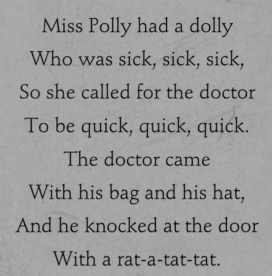

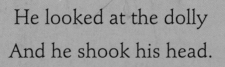

Miss Polly had a dolly
Who was sick, sick, sick,
So she called for the doctor
To be quick, quick, quick.
The doctor came
With his bag and his hat,
And he knocked at the door
With a rat-a-tat-tat.

He looked at the dolly
And he shook his head.
He said, "Miss Polly, put her straight to bed."
He wrote out a paper
For a pill, pill, pill.
"I'll be back in the morning
With my bill, bill, bill."

Pussycat, Pussycat

Pussycat, pussycat, where have you been?

I've been up to London to visit the Queen.

Pussycat, pussycat, what did you there?

I frightened a little mouse under her chair.

MIAOW!

Mary, Mary Quite Contrary

Mary, Mary quite contrary,
How does your garden grow?
With silver bells, and cockle shells,
And pretty maids all in a row.